RAYMOND
CHANDLER

GOLDFISH

PENGUIN BOOKS

PENGUIN BOOKS

Published by the Penguin Group. Penguin Books Ltd, 27 Wrights Lane, London
W8 5TZ, England. Penguin Books USA Inc., 375 Hudson Street, New York, New
York 10014, USA. Penguin Books Australia Ltd, Ringwood, Victoria, Australia.
Penguin Books Canada Ltd, 10 Alcorn Avenue, Toronto, Ontario, Canada M4V 3B2.
Penguin Books (NZ) Ltd, 182–190 Wairau Road, Auckland 10, New Zealand ·
Penguin Books Ltd, Registered Offices: Harmondsworth, Middlesex, England ·
This story has been taken from *Trouble is My Business* **by Raymond
Chandler, published by Penguin Books in 1950.** This edition published 1995 ·
This selection copyright 1950 by Penguin Books Ltd. All rights reserved · Typeset
by Datix International Limited, Bungay, Suffolk · Printed in England by Clays
Ltd, St Ives plc · Except in the United States of America, this book is sold subject
to the condition that it shall not, by way of trade or otherwise, be lent, re-sold,
hired out, or otherwise circulated without the publisher's prior consent in any form
of binding or cover other than that in which it is published and without a similar
condition including this condition being imposed on the subsequent purchaser ·
10 9 8 7 6 5 4 3 2 1

I wasn't doing any work that day, just catching up on my foot-dangling. A warm gusty breeze was blowing in at the office window and the soot from the *Mansion House Hotel* oil-burners across the alley was rolling across the glass top of my desk in tiny particles, like pollen drifting over a vacant lot.

I was just thinking about going to lunch when Kathy Horne came in.

She was a tall, seedy, sad-eyed blonde who had once been a policewoman and had lost her job when she married a cheap little check-bouncer named Johnny Horne, to reform him. She hadn't reformed him, but she was waiting for him to come out so she could try again. In the meantime she ran the cigar counter at the *Mansion House*, and watched the grifters go by in a haze of nickel cigar smoke. And once in a while lent one of them ten dollars to get out of town. She was just that soft. She sat down and opened her big shiny bag and got out a package of cigarettes and lit one with my desk lighter. She blew a plume of smoke, wrinkled her nose at it.

'Did you ever hear of the Leander pearls?' she asked. 'Gosh, that blue serge shines. You must have money in the bank, the clothes you wear.'

'No,' I said, 'to both your ideas. I never heard of the Leander pearls and don't have any money in the bank.'

'Then you'd like to make yourself a cut of twenty-five grand maybe.'

I lit one of her cigarettes. She got up and shut the window, saying: 'I get enough of that hotel smell on the job.'

She sat down again, went on:

'It's nineteen years ago. They had the guy in Leavenworth fifteen and it's four since they let him out. A big lumberman from up north named Sol Leander bought them for his wife – the pearls, I mean – just two of them. They cost two hundred grand.'

'It must have taken a hand truck to move them,' I said.

'I see you don't know a lot about pearls,' Kathy Horne said. 'It's not just size. Anyhow they're worth more today and the twenty-five-grand reward the Reliance people put out is still good.'

'I get it,' I said. 'Somebody copped them off.'

'Now you're getting yourself some oxygen.' She dropped her cigarette into a tray and let it smoke, as ladies will. I put it out for her. 'That's what the guy was in Leavenworth for, only they never proved he got the pearls. It was a mail-car job. He got himself hidden in the car somehow and up in Wyoming he shot the clerk, cleaned out the registered mail and dropped off. He got to B.C. before he was nailed. But they didn't get any of the stuff – not then. All they got was him. He got life.'

'If it's going to be a long story, let's have a drink.'

'I never drink until sundown. That way you don't get to be a heel.'

2

'Tough on the Eskimos,' I said. 'In the summertime, anyway.'

She watched me get my little flat bottle out. Then she went on:

'His name was Sype – Wally Sype. He did it alone. And he wouldn't squawk about the stuff, not a peep. Then after fifteen long years they offered him a pardon, if he would loosen up with the loot. He gave up everything but the pearls.'

'Where did he have it?' I asked. 'In his hat?'

'Listen, this isn't just a bunch of gag lines. I've got a lead to those marbles.'

I shut my mouth with my hand and looked solemn.

'He said he never had the pearls and they must have halfway believed him because they gave him the pardon. Yet the pearls were in the load, registered mail, and they were never seen again.'

My throat began to feel a little thick. I didn't say anything.

Kathy Horne went on:

'One time in Leavenworth, just one time in all those years, Wally Sype wrapped himself around a can of white shellac and got as tight as a fat lady's girdle. His cell mate was a little man they called Peeler Mardo. He was doing twenty-seven months for splitting twenty dollar bills. Sype told him he had the pearls buried somewhere in Idaho.'

I leaned forward a little.

'Beginning to get to you, eh?' she said. 'Well get this. Peeler Mardo is rooming at my house and he's a coke-hound and he talks in his sleep.'

3

I leaned back again. 'Good grief,' I said. 'And I was practically spending the reward money.'

She stared at me coldly. Then her face softened. 'All right,' she said a little hopelessly. 'I know it sounds screwy. All those years gone by and all the smart heads that must have worked on the case, postal men and private agencies and all. And then a coke-head to turn it up. But he's a nice little runt and somehow I believe him. He knows where Sype is.'

I said: 'Did he talk all this in his sleep?'

'Of course not. But you know me. An old policewoman's got ears. Maybe I was nosy, but I guessed he was an ex-con and I worried about him using the stuff so much. He's the only roomer I've got now and I'd kind of go in by his door and listen to him talking to himself. That way I got enough to brace him. He told me the rest. He wants help to collect.'

I leaned forward again. 'Where's Sype?'

Kathy Horne smiled, and shook her head. 'That's the one thing he wouldn't tell, that and the name Sype is using now. But it's somewhere up north, in or near Olympia, Washington. Peeler saw him up there and found out about him and he says Sype didn't see *him*.'

'What's Peeler doing down here?' I asked.

'Here's where they put the Leavenworth rap on him. You know an old con always goes back to look at the piece of sidewalk he slipped on. But he doesn't have any friends here now.'

I lit another cigarette and had another little drink.

'Sype has been out four years, you say. Peeler did twenty-seven months. What's he been doing with all the time since?'

Kathy Horne widened her china blue eyes pityingly. 'Maybe you think there's only one jailhouse he could get into.'

'Okay,' I said. 'Will he talk to me? I guess he wants help to deal with the insurance people, in case there are any pearls and Sype will put them right in Peeler's hand and so on. Is that it?'

Kathy Horne sighed. 'Yes, he'll talk to you. He's aching to. He's scared about something. Will you go out now, before he gets junked up for the evening?'

'Sure – if that's what you want.'

She took a flat key out of her bag and wrote an address on my pad. She stood up slowly.

'It's a double house. My side's separate. There's a door in between, with the key on my side. That's just in case he won't come to the door.'

'Okay,' I said. I blew smoke at the ceiling and stared at her.

She went towards the door, stopped, came back. She looked down at the floor.

'I don't rate much in it,' she said. 'Maybe not anything. But if I could have a grand or two waiting for Johnny when he came out, maybe –'

'Maybe you could hold him straight,' I said. 'It's a dream, Kathy. It's all a dream. But if it isn't you cut an even third.'

She caught her breath and glared at me to keep from crying. She went towards the door, stopped and came back again.

'That isn't all,' she said. 'It's the old guy – Sype. He did 5 fifteen years. He paid. Paid hard. Doesn't it make you feel kind of mean?'

I shook my head. 'He stole them, didn't he? He killed a man. What does he do for a living?'

'His wife has money,' Kathy Horne said. 'He just plays around with goldfish.'

'Goldfish?' I said. 'To hell with him.'

She went on out.

2

The last time I had been in the Gray Lake district I had helped a D.A.'s man named Bernie Obis shoot a gunman named Poke Andrews. But that was higher up the hill, further away from the lake. This house was on the second level, in a loop the street made rounding a spur of the hill. It stood by itself high up, with a cracked retaining wall in front and several vacant lots behind.

Being originally a double house it had two front doors and two sets of front steps. One of the doors had a sign tacked over the grating that masked the peep window: Ring 1432.

I parked my car and went up right-angle steps, passed between two lines of pinks, went up more steps to the side with the sign. That should be the roomer's side. I rang the bell. Nobody answered it, so I went across to the other door. Nobody answered that one either.

While I was waiting a grey Dodge coupé whished around the curve and a small neat girl in blue looked up at me for a second. I didn't see who else was in the car. I didn't pay much attention. I didn't know it was important.

I took out Kathy Horne's key and let myself into a closed living-room that smelled of cedar oil. There was just enough furniture to get by, net curtains, a quiet shaft of sunlight under the drapes in front. There was a tiny breakfast room, a kitchen, a bedroom in the back that was obviously Kathy's, a bathroom, another bedroom in front that seemed to be used as a sewing-room. It was this room that had the door cut through to the other side of the house.

I unlocked it and stepped, as it were, through a mirror. Everything was backwards, except the furniture. The living-room on that side had twin beds, didn't have the look of being lived in.

I went towards the back of the house, past the second bathroom, knocked at the shut door that corresponded to Kathy's bedroom.

No answer. I tried the knob and went in. The little man on the bed was probably Peeler Mardo. I noticed his feet first, because although he had on trousers and a shirt, his feet were bare and hung over the end of the bed. They were tied there by a rope around the ankles.

They had been burned raw on the soles. There was a smell of scorched flesh in spite of the open window. Also a smell of scorched wood. An electric iron on a desk was still connected. I went over and shut it off.

I went back to Kathy Horne's kitchen and found a pint of Brooklyn Scotch in the cooler. I used some of it and breathed deeply for a little while and looked out over the vacant lots. 7

There was a narrow cement walk behind the house and green wooden steps down to the street.

I went back to Peeler Mardo's room. The coat of a brown suit with a red pin stripe hung over a chair with the pockets turned out and what had been in them on the floor.

He was wearing the trousers of the suit, and their pockets were turned out also. Some keys and change and a handkerchief lay on the bed beside him, and a metal box like a woman's compact, from which some glistening white powder had spilled. Cocaine.

He was a little man, not more than five feet four, with thin brown hair and large ears. His eyes had no particular colour. They were just eyes, and very wide open, and quite dead. His arms were pulled out from him and tied at the wrists by a rope that went under the bed.

I looked him over for bullet or knife wounds, didn't find any. There wasn't a mark on him except his feet. Shock or heart failure or a combination of the two must have done the trick. He was still warm. The gag in his mouth was both warm and wet.

I wiped off everything I had touched, looked out of Kathy's front window for a while before I left the house.

It was three-thirty when I walked into the lobby of the *Mansion House*, over to the cigar counter in the corner. I leaned on the glass and asked for Camels.

Kathy Horne flicked the pack at me, dropped the change into my outside breast pocket, and gave me her customer's smile.

'Well? You didn't take long,' she said, and looked side-wise along her eyes at a drunk who was trying to light a cigar with the old-fashioned flint and steel lighter.

'It's heavy,' I told her. 'Get set.'

She turned away quickly and flipped a pack of paper matches along the glass to the drunk. He fumbled for them, dropped both matches and cigar, scooped them angrily off the floor and went off looking back over his shoulder, as if he expected a kick.

Kathy looked past my head, her eyes cool and empty.

'I'm set,' she whispered.

'You cut a full half,' I said. 'Peeler's out. He's been bumped off – in his bed.'

Her eyes twitched. Two fingers curled on the glass near my elbow. A white line showed around her mouth. That was all.

'Listen,' I said. 'Don't say anything until I'm through. He died of shock. Somebody burned his feet with a cheap electric iron. Not yours. I looked. I'd say he died rather quickly and couldn't have said much. The gag was still in his mouth. When I went out there, frankly, I thought it was all hooey. Now I'm not so sure. If he gave up his dope, we're through, and so is Sype, unless I can find him first. Those workers didn't have any inhibitions at all. If he didn't give up, there's still time.'

Her head turned, her set eyes looked towards the revolving door of the lobby entrance. White patches glared in her cheeks.

'What do I do?' she breathed.

I poked at a box of wrapped cigars, dropped her key into it. Her long fingers got it out smoothly, hid it.

'When you get home you find him. You don't know a thing. Leave the pearls out, leave me out. When they check his prints they'll know he had a record and they'll just figure it was something caught up with him.'

I broke my cigarettes open and lit one, watched her for a moment. She didn't move an inch.

'Can you face it down?' I asked. 'If you can't, now's the time to speak.'

'Of course.' Her eyebrows arched. 'Do I look like a torturer?'

'You married a crook,' I said grimly.

She flushed, which was what I wanted. 'He isn't! He's just a damn fool! Nobody thinks any the worse of me, not even the boys down at Headquarters.'

'All right. I like it that way. It's not our murder, after all. And if we talk now, you can say good-bye to any share in any reward – even if one is ever paid.'

'Darn tootin',' Kathy Horne said pertly. 'Oh, the poor little runt,' she almost sobbed.

I patted her arm, grinned as heartily as I could and left the *Mansion House*.

3

The Reliance Indemnity Company had offices in the Graas Building, three small rooms that looked like nothing at all. They were a big enough outfit to be as shabby as they liked.

The resident manager was named Lutin, a middle-aged bald-headed man with quiet eyes, dainty fingers that caressed a dappled cigar. He sat behind a large, well-dusted desk and stared peacefully at my chin.

'Carmady, eh? I've heard of you.' He touched my card with a shiny little finger. 'What's on your mind?'

I rolled a cigarette around in my fingers and lowered my voice. 'Remember the Leander pearls?'

His smile was slow, a little bored. 'I'm not likely to forget them. They cost this company one hundred and fifty thousand dollars. I was a cocky young adjuster then.'

I said: 'I've got an idea. It may be all haywire. It very likely is. But I'd like to try it out. Is your twenty-five-grand reward still good?'

He chuckled. 'Twenty grand, Carmady. We spent the difference ourselves. You're wasting time.'

'It's my time. Twenty it is then. How much cooperation can I get?'

'What kind of cooperation?'

'Can I have a letter identifying me to your other branches? In case I have to go out of the State. In case I need kind words from some local law.'

'Which way out of the State?'

I smiled at him. He tapped his cigar on the edge of a tray and smiled back. Neither of our smiles was honest.

'No letter,' he said. 'New York wouldn't stand for it. We have our own tie-up. But all the cooperation you can use, under the hat. And the twenty grand, if you click. Of course you won't.'

I lit my cigarette and leaned back, puffed smoke at the ceiling.

'No? Why not? You never got those marbles. They existed, didn't they?'

'Darn right they existed. And if they still do, they belong to us. But two hundred grand doesn't get buried for twenty years – and then get dug up.'

'All right. It's still my own time.'

He knocked a little ash off his cigar and looked down his eyes at me. 'I like your front,' he said, 'even if you are crazy. But we're a large organization. Suppose I have you covered from now on. What then?'

'I lose. I'll know I'm covered. I'm too long in the game to miss that. I'll quit, give up what I know to the law, and go home.'

'Why would you do that?'

I leaned forward over the desk again. 'Because,' I said slowly, 'the guy that had the lead got bumped off today.'

'Oh – oh.' Lutin rubbed his nose.

'I didn't bump him off,' I added.

We didn't talk any more for a little while. Then Lutin said:

'You don't want any letter. You wouldn't even carry it. And after your telling me that, you know damn well I won't dare give it to you.'

I stood up, grinned, started for the door. He got up himself, very fast, ran around the desk and put his small neat hand on my arm.

'Listen, I know you're crazy, but if you do get anything, bring it in through our boys. We need the advertising.'

'What the hell do you think I live on?' I growled.

'Twenty-five grand.'

'I thought it was twenty.'

'Twenty-five. And you're still crazy. Sype never had those pearls. If he had, he'd have made some kind of terms with us many years ago.'

'Okay,' I said. 'You've had plenty of time to make up your mind.'

We shook hands, grinned at each other like a couple of wise boys who know they're not kidding anybody, but won't give up trying.

It was a quarter to five when I got back to the office. I had a couple of short drinks and stuffed a pipe and sat down to interview my brains. The phone rang.

A woman's voice said: 'Carmady?' It was a small, tight, cold voice. I didn't know it.

'Yeah.'

'Better see Rush Madder. Know him?'

'No,' I lied. 'Why should I see him?'

There was a sudden tinkling, icy-cold laugh on the wire. 'On account of a guy had sore feet,' the voice said.

The phone clicked. I put my end of it aside, struck a match and stared at the wall until the flame burned my fingers.

Rush Madder was a shyster in the Quorn Building. An ambulance chaser, a small time fixer, an alibi builder-upper, anything that smelled a little and paid a little more. I hadn't heard of him in connexion with any big operations like burning people's feet.

4

It was getting toward quitting time on lower Spring Street. Taxis were dawdling close to the kerb, stenographers were getting an early start home, street cars were clogging up, and traffic cops were preventing people from making perfectly legal right turns.

The Quorn Building was a narrow front, the colour of dried mustard, with a large case of false teeth in the entrance. The directory held the names of painless dentists, people who teach you how to become a letter-carrier, just names, and numbers without any names. Rush Madder, Attorney-at-Law, was in Room 619.

I got out of a jolting open cage elevator, looked at a dirty spittoon on a dirty rubber mat, walked down a corridor that smelled of butts, and tried the knob below the frosted glass panel of 619. The door was locked. I knocked.

A shadow came against the glass and the door was pulled back with a squeak. I was looking at a thick-set man with a soft round chin, heavy black eyebrows, an oily complexion, and a Charlie Chan moustache that made his face look fatter than it was.

He put out a couple of nicotined fingers. 'Well, well, the old dog-catcher himself. The eye that never forgets. Carmady is the name, I believe?'

I stepped inside and waited for the door to squeak shut. A bare carpetless room paved in brown linoleum, a flat desk and a rolltop at right angles to it, a big green safe that looked as fireproof as a delicatessen bag, two filing cases, three chairs, a built-in closet, and washbowl in the corner by the door.

'Well, well, sit down,' Madder said. 'Glad to see you.' He fussed around behind his desk and adjusted a burst-out seat cushion, sat on it. 'Nice of you to drop around. Business?'

I sat down and put a cigarette between my teeth and looked at him. I didn't say a word. I watched him start to sweat. It started up in his hair. Then he grabbed a pencil and made marks on his blotter. Then he looked at me with a quick darting glance, down at his blotter again. He talked – to the blotter.

'Any ideas?' he asked softly.

'About what?'

He didn't look at me. 'About how we could do a little business together. Say, in stones.'

'Who was the wren?' I asked.

'Huh? What wren?' He still didn't look at me.

'The one that phoned me.'

'Did somebody phone you?'

I reached for his telephone, which was the old-fashioned gallows type. I lifted off the receiver and started to dial the number of Police Headquarters, very slowly. I knew he would know that number about as well as he knew his hat.

He reached over and pushed the hook down. 'Now, listen,' he complained. 'You're too fast. What you calling coppers for?'

I said slowly: 'They want to talk to you. On account of you know a broad that knows a man had sore feet.'

15

'Does it have to be that way?' His collar was too tight now. He yanked at it.

'Not from my side. But if you think I'm going to sit here and let you play with my reflexes, it does.'

Madder opened a flat tin of cigarettes and pushed one past his lips with a sound like somebody gutting a fish. His hand shook.

'All right,' he said thickly. 'All right. Don't get sore.'

'Just stop trying to count clouds with me,' I growled. 'Talk sense. If you've got a job for me, it's probably too dirty for me to touch. But I'll at least listen.'

He nodded. He was comfortable now. He knew I was bluffing. He puffed a pale swirl of smoke and watched it float up.

'That's all right,' he said evenly. 'I play dumb myself once in a while. The thing is we're wise. Carol saw you go to the house and leave it again. No law came.'

'Carol?'

'Carol Donovan. Friend of mine. She called you up.'

I nodded. 'Go ahead.'

He didn't say anything. He just sat there and looked at me owlishly.

I grinned and leaned across the desk a little and said: 'Here's what's bothering you. You don't know why I went to the house or why, having gone, I didn't yell police. That's easy. I thought it was a secret.'

'We're just kidding each other,' Madder said sourly.

'All right,' I said. 'Let's talk about pearls. Does that make it any easier?'

His eyes shone. He wanted to let himself get excited, but he didn't. He kept his voice down, said coolly:

'Carol picked him up one night, the little guy. A crazy little number, full of snow, but way back in his noodle an idea. He'd talk about pearls, about an old guy up in the northwest of Canada that swiped them a long time ago and still had them. Only he wouldn't say who the old guy was or where he was. Foxy about that. Holding out. I wouldn't know why.'

'He wanted to get his feet burned,' I said.

Madder's lips shook and another fine sweat showed in his hair.

'I didn't do that,' he said thickly.

'You or Carol, what's the odds? The little guy died. They can make murder out of it. You didn't find out what you wanted to know. That's why *I'm* here. You think I have information you didn't get. Forget it. If I knew enough, I wouldn't be here, and if you knew enough, you wouldn't want me here. Check?'

He grinned, very slowly, as if it hurt him. He struggled up in his chair and dragged a deep drawer out from the side of his desk, put a nicely moulded brown bottle up on the desk, and two striped glasses. He whispered:

'Two way split. You and me. I'm cutting Carol out. She's too damn rough, Carmady. I've seen hard women, but she's the blueing on armour plate. And you'd never think it to look at her, would you?'

'Have I seen her?'

'I guess so. She says you did.'

'Oh, the girl in the Dodge.'

He nodded, and poured two good-sized drinks, put the bottle down and stood up. 'Water? I like it in mine.'

'No,' I said, 'but why cut me in? I don't know any more than you mentioned. Or very little. Certainly not as much as you must know to go that far.'

He leered across the glasses. 'I know where I can get fifty grand for the Leander pearls, twice what you could get. I can give you yours and still have mine. You've got the front I need to work in the open. How about the water?'

'No water,' I said.

He went across to the built-in wash place and ran the water and came back with his glass half full. He sat down again, grinned, lifted it.

We drank.

5

So far I had only made four mistakes. The first was mixing in it at all, even for Kathy Horne's sake. The second was staying mixed after I found Peeler Mardo dead. The third was letting Rush Madder see I knew what he was talking about. The fourth, the whisky, was the worst.

It tasted funny even on the way down. Then there was that sudden moment of sharp lucidity when I knew, exactly as though I had seen it, that he had switched his drink for a harmless one cached in the closet.

I sat still for a moment, with the empty glass at my

fingers' ends, gathering my strength. Madder's face began to get large and moony and vague. A fat smile jerked in and out under his Charlie Chan moustache as he watched me.

I reached back into my hip pocket and pulled out a loosely wadded handkerchief. The small safe inside it didn't seem to show. At least Madder didn't move, after his first grab under the coat.

I stood up and swayed forward drunkenly and smacked him square on the top of the head.

He gagged. He started to get up. I tapped him on the jaw. He became limp and his hand sweeping down from under his coat knocked his glass over on the desk top. I straightened it, stood silent, listening, struggling with a rising wave of nauseous stupor.

I went over to a communicating door and tried the knob. It was locked. I was staggering by now. I dragged an office chair to the entrance door and propped the back of it under the knob. I leaned against the door panting, gritting my teeth, cursing myself. I got handcuffs out and started back towards Madder.

A very pretty black-haired, grey-eyed girl stepped out of the clothes closet and poked a .32 at me.

She wore a blue suit cut with a lot of snap. An inverted saucer of a hat came down in a hard line across her forehead. Shiny black hair showed at the sides. Her eyes were slate-grey, cold, and yet light-hearted. Her face was fresh and young and delicate and as hard as a chisel.

'All right, Carmady. Lie down and sleep it off. You're through.'

I stumbled towards her waving my sap. She shook her head. When her face moved it got large before my eyes. Its outlines changed and wobbled. The gun in her hand looked like anything from a tunnel to a toothpick.

'Don't be a goof, Carmady,' she said. 'A few hours' sleep for you, a few hours' start for us. Don't make me shoot. I would.'

'Damn you,' I mumbled. 'I believe you would.'

'Right as rain, toots. I'm a lady that wants her own way. That's fine. Sit down.'

The floor rose up and bumped me. I sat on it as on a raft in a rough sea. I braced myself on flat hands. I could hardly feel the floor. My hands were numb. My whole body was numb.

I tried to stare her down. 'Ha-a! L-lady K-killer!' I giggled.

She threw a chilly laugh at me which I only just barely heard. Drums were beating in my head now, war drums from a far off jungle. Waves of light were moving, and dark shadows and a rustle as of a wind in tree-tops. I didn't want to lie down. I lay down.

The girl's voice came from very far off, an elfin voice.

'Two-way split, eh? He doesn't like my method, eh? Bless his big soft heart. We'll see about him.'

Vaguely as I floated off I seemed to feel a dull jar that might have been a shot. I hoped she had shot Madder, but she hadn't. She had merely helped me on my way out – with my own sap.

When I came around again it was night. Something clacked overhead with a heavy sound. Through the open window beyond the desk yellow light splashed on the high side walls of a building. The thing clacked again and the light went off. An advertising sign on the roof.

I got up off the floor like a man climbing out of thick mud. I waded over to the washbowl, splashed water on my face, felt the top of my head and winced, waded back to the door and found the light switch.

Strewn papers lay around the desk, broken pencils, envelopes, an empty brown whisky bottle, cigarette ends, and ashes. The debris of hastily emptied drawers. I didn't bother going through any of it. I left the office, rode down to the street in the shuddering elevator, slid into a bar and had a brandy, then got my car and drove on home.

I changed clothes, packed a bag, had some whisky, and answered the telephone. It was about nine-thirty.

Kathy Horne's voice said: 'So you're not gone yet. I hoped you wouldn't be.'

'Alone?' I asked, still thick in the voice.

'Yes, but I haven't been. The house has been full of coppers for hours. They were very nice, considering. Old grudge of some kind, they figured.'

'And the line is likely tapped now,' I growled. 'Where was I supposed to be going?'

'Well – you know. Your girl told me.'

'Little dark girl? Very cool? Name of Carol Donovan?'

'She had your card. Why, wasn't it –'

'I don't have any girl,' I said simply. 'And I bet that just very casually, without thinking at all a name slipped past your lips – the name of a town up north. Did it?'

'Ye-es,' Kathy Horne admitted weakly.

I caught the night plane north.

It was a nice trip except that I had a sore head and a raging thirst for ice-water.

6

The *Snoqualmie Hotel* in Olympia was on Capitol Way, fronting on the usual square city block of park. I left by the coffee shop door and walked down a hill to where the last, loneliest reach of Puget Sound dried and decomposed against a line of disused wharves. Corded firewood filled the foreground and old men pottered about in the middle of the stacks, or sat on boxes with pipes in their mouths and signs behind their heads reading: 'Firewood and Split Kindling. Free Delivery.'

Behind them a low cliff rose and the vast pines of the north loomed against a grey-blue sky.

Two of the old men sat on boxes about twenty feet apart, ignoring each other. I drifted near one of them. He wore corduroy pants and what had been a red and black mackinaw. His felt hat showed the sweat of twenty summers. One of his hands clutched a short black pipe, and with the grimed fingers of the other he slowly, carefully, ecstatically jerked at a long curling hair that grew out of his nose.

I set a box on end, sat down, filled my own pipe, lit it, puffed a cloud of smoke. I waved a hand at the water and said:

22

'You'd never think that ever met the Pacific Ocean.'

He looked at me.

I said: 'Dead end – quiet, restful, like your town. I like a town like this.' He went on looking at me.

'I'll bet,' I said, 'that a man that's been around a town like this knows everybody in it and in the country near it.'

He said: 'How much you bet?'

I took a silver dollar out of my pocket. They still had a few up there. The old man looked it over, nodded, suddenly yanked the long hair out of his nose and held it up against the light.

'You'd lose,' he said.

I put the dollar down on my knee. 'Know anybody around here that keeps a lot of goldfish?' I asked.

He stared at the dollar. The other old man near by was wearing overalls and shoes without any laces. He stared at the dollar. They both spat at the same instant. The first old man turned his head and yelled at the top of his voice:

'Know anybody keeps goldfish?'

The other old man jumped up off his box and seized a big axe, set a log on end and whanged the axe down on it, splitting it evenly. He looked at the first old man triumphantly and screamed:

'I ain't neither.'

The first old man said: 'Leetle deef.' He got up slowly and went over to a shack built of old boards of uneven lengths. He went into it, banged the door.

The second old man threw his axe down pettishly, spat in the direction of the closed door and went off among the stacks of cordwood.

The door of the shack opened, the man in the mackinaw poked his head out of it.

'Sewer crabs is all,' he said, and slammed the door again.

I put my dollar in my pocket and went back up the hill. I figured it would take too long to learn their language.

Capitol Way ran north and south. A dull green street car shuttled past on the way to a place called Tumwater. In the distance I could see the government buildings. Northward the street passed two hotels and some stores and branched right and left. Right went to Tacoma and Seattle. Left went over a bridge and out on to the Olympic Peninsula.

Beyond this right and left turn the street suddenly became old and shabby, with broken asphalt paving, a Chinese restaurant, a boarded-up movie house, a pawnbroker's establishment. A sign jutting over the dirty sidewalk said: 'Smoke Shop', and in small letters underneath, as if it hoped nobody was looking, 'Pool'.

I went in past a rack of gaudy magazines and a cigar showcase that had flies inside it. There was a long wooden counter on the left, a few slot machines, a single pool table. Three kids fiddled with the slot machines and a tall thin man with a long nose and no chin played pool all by himself, with a dead cigar in his face.

I sat on a stool and a hard-eyed bald-headed man behind the counter got up from a chair, wiped his hands on a thick grey apron, showed me a gold tooth.

'A little rye,' I said. 'Know anybody that keeps goldfish?'

'Yeah,' he said. 'No.'

He poured something behind the counter and shoved a thick glass across.

'Two bits.'

I sniffed the stuff, wrinkled my nose. 'Was it the rye the "yeah" was for?'

The bald-headed man held up a large bottle with a label that said something about: 'Cream of Dixie Straight Rye Whiskey Guaranteed at Least Four Months Old.'

'Okay,' I said. 'I see it just moved in.'

I poured some water in it and drank it. It tasted like a cholera culture. I put a quarter on the counter. The barman showed me a gold tooth on the other side of his face and took hold of the counter with two hard hands and pushed his chin at me.

'What was that crack?' he asked, almost gently.

'I just moved in,' I said. 'I'm looking for some goldfish for the front window. Goldfish.'

The barman said very slowly: 'Do I look like a guy would know a guy would have goldfish?' His face was a little white.

The long-nosed man who had been playing himself a round of pool racked his cue and strolled over to the counter beside me and threw a nickel on it.

'Draw me a drink before you wet yourself,' he told the barman.

The barman prised himself loose from the counter with a good deal of effort. I looked down to see if his fingers had made any dents in the wood. He drew a coke, stirred it with a swizzle-stick, dumped it on the bar top, took a deep breath 25 and let it out through his nose, grunted and went away towards a door marked: 'Toilet'.

The long-nosed man lifted his coke and looked into the smeared mirror behind the bar. The left side of his mouth twitched briefly. A dim voice came from it, saying:

'How's Peeler?'

I pressed my thumb and forefinger together, put them to my nose, sniffed, shook my head sadly.

'Hitting it high, huh?'

'Yeah,' I said. 'I didn't catch the name.'

'Call me Sunset. I'm always movin' west. Think he'll stay clammed?'

'He'll stay clammed,' I said.

'What's your handle?'

'Dodge Willis, El Paso,' I said.

'Got a room somewhere?'

'Hotel.'

He put his glass down empty. 'Let's dangle.'

7

We went up to my room and sat down and looked at each other over a couple of glasses of Scotch and ginger ale. Sunset studied me with his close-set expressionless eyes, a little at a time, but very thoroughly in the end, adding it all up.

I sipped my drink and waited. At last he said in his lipless 'stir' voice:

'How come Peeler didn't come hisself?'

'For the same reason he didn't stay when he was here.'

'Meaning which?'

'Figure it out for yourself,' I said.

He nodded, just as though I had said something with a meaning. Then:

'What's the top price?'

'Twenty-five grand.'

'Nuts.' Sunset was emphatic, even rude.

I leaned back and lit a cigarette, puffed smoke at the open window and watched the breeze pick it up and tear it to pieces.

'Listen,' Sunset complained. 'I don't know you from last Sunday's sports section. You may be all to the silk. I just don't know.'

'Why'd you brace me?' I asked.

'You had the word, didn't you?'

This was where I took the dive. I grinned at him. 'Yeah. Goldfish was the password. The *Smoke Shop* was the place.'

His lack of expression told me I was right. It was one of those breaks you dream of, but don't handle right even in dreams.

'Well, what's the next angle?' Sunset inquired, sucking a piece of ice out of his glass and chewing on it.

I laughed. 'Okay, Sunset. I'm satisfied you're cagey. We could go on like this for weeks. Let's put our cards on the table. Where is the old guy?'

Sunset tightened his lips, moistened them, tightened them 27 again. He set his glass down very slowly and his right hand hung lax on his thigh. I knew I had made a mistake, that Peeler knew where the old guy was, exactly. Therefore I should know.

Nothing in Sunset's voice showed I had made a mistake. He said crossly: 'You mean why don't I put my cards on the table and you just sit back and look 'em over. Nix.'

'Then how do you like this?' I growled. 'Peeler's dead.'

One eyebrow twitched, and one corner of his mouth. His eyes got a little blanker than before, if possible. His voice rasped lightly, like a finger on dry leather.

'How come?'

'Competition you two didn't know about.' I leaned back, smiled.

The gun made a soft metallic blur in the sunshine. I hardly saw where it came from. Then the muzzle was round and dark and empty looking at me.

'You're kidding the wrong guy,' Sunset said lifelessly. 'I ain't no soft spot for chiselers to lie on.'

I folded my arms, taking care that my right hand was outside, in view.

'I would be – if I was kidding. I'm not. Peeler played with a girl and she milked him – up to a point. He didn't tell her where to find the old fellow. So she and her top man went to see Peeler where he lived. They used a hot iron on his feet. He died of the shock.'

Sunset looked unimpressed. 'I got a lot of room in my ears yet,' he said.

'So have I,' I snarled, suddenly pretending anger. 'Just

what the hell have you said that means anything – except that you know Peeler?'

He spun his gun on his trigger finger, watching it spin. 'Old man Sype's at Westport,' he said casually. 'That mean anything to you?'

'Yeah. Has he got the marbles?'

'How the hell would I know?' He steadied the gun again, dropped it to his thigh. It wasn't pointing at me now. 'Where's this competish you mentioned?'

'I hoped I ditched them,' I said. 'I'm not too sure. Can I put my hands down and take a drink?'

'Yeah, go ahead. How did you cut in?'

'Peeler roomed with the wife of a friend of mine who's in stir. A straight girl, one you can trust. He let her in and she passed it to me – afterwards.'

'After the bump? How many cuts your side? My half is set.'

I took my drink, shoved the empty glass away. 'The hell it is.'

The gun lifted an inch, dropped again. 'How many altogether?' he snapped.

'Three, now Peeler's out. If we can hold off the competition.'

'The feet-toasters? No trouble about that. What they look like?'

'Man named Rush Madder, a shyster down south, fifty, fat, thin down-curving moustache, dark hair thin on top, five-nine, a hundred and eighty, not much guts. The girl, Carol Donovan, black hair, long bob, grey eyes, pretty, small 29 features, twenty-five to eight, five-two, hundred twenty, last seen wearing blue, hard as they come. The real iron in the combination.'

Sunset nodded indifferently and put his gun away. 'We'll soften her, if she pokes her snoot in,' he said. 'I've got a heap at the house. Let's take the air Westport way and look it over. You might be able to ease in on the goldfish angle. They say he's nuts about them. I'll stay under cover. He's too stir-wise for me. I smell of the bucket.'

'Swell,' I said heartily. 'I'm an old goldfish fancier myself.'

Sunset reached for the bottle, poured two fingers of Scotch and put it down. He stood up, twitched his collar straight, then shot his chinless jaw forward as far as it would go.

'But don't make no error, bo. It's goin' to take pressure. It's goin' to mean a run out in the deep woods and some thumb twisting. Snatch stuff, likely.'

'That's okay,' I said. 'The insurance people are behind us.'

Sunset jerked down the points of his vest and rubbed the back of his thin neck. I put my hat on, locked the Scotch in the bag by the chair I'd been sitting in, went over and shut the window.

We started towards the door. Knuckles rattled on it just as I reached for the knob. I gestured Sunset back along the wall. I stared at the door for a moment and then I opened it up.

The two guns came forward almost on the same level, one small — a .32, one a big Smith and Wesson. They couldn't come into the room abreast, so the girl came in first.

'Okay, hot shot,' she said dryly. 'Ceiling zero. See if you can reach it.'

8

I backed slowly into the room. The two visitors bored in on me, either side. I tripped over my bag and fell backwards, hit the floor and rolled on my side groaning.

Sunset said casually: 'H'ist 'm, folks. Pretty now!'

Two heads jerked away from looking down at me and then I had my gun loose, down at my side. I kept on groaning.

There was a silence. I didn't hear any guns fall. The door of the room was still wide open and Sunset was flattened against the wall more or less behind it.

The girl said between her teeth: 'Cover the shamus, Rush – and shut the door. Skinny can't shoot here. Nobody can.' Then, in a whisper I barely caught, she added: 'Slam it!'

Rush Madder waddled backwards across the room keeping the Smith and Wesson pointed my way. His back was to Sunset and the thought of that made his eyes roll. I could have shot him easily enough, but it wasn't the play. Sunset stood with his feet spread and his tongue showing. Something that could have been a smile wrinkled his flat eyes.

He stared at the girl and she stared at him. Their guns stared at each other.

Rush Madder reached the door, grabbed the edge of it and gave it a hard swing. I knew exactly what was going to happen. As the door slammed the .32 was going to go off. It wouldn't be heard if it went off at the right instant. The explosion would be lost in the slamming of the door.

I reached out and took hold of Carol Donovan's ankle and jerked it hard.

The door slammed. Her gun went off and chipped the ceiling.

She whirled on me kicking. Sunset said in his tight but somehow penetrating drawl:

'If this is it, this is it. Let's go!' The hammer clicked back on his Colt.

Something in his voice steadied Carol Donovan. She relaxed, let her automatic fall to her side and stepped away from me with a vicious look back.

Madder turned the key in the door and leaned against the wood, breathing noisily. His hat had tipped over one ear and the end of two strips of adhesive showed under the brim.

Nobody moved while I had these thoughts. There was no sound of feet outside in the hall, no alarm, I got up on my knees, slid my gun out of sight, rose on my feet and went over to the window. Nobody down on the sidewalk was staring up at the upper floors of the *Snoqualmie Hotel*.

I sat on the broad old-fashioned sill and looked faintly embarrassed, as though the minister had said a bad word.

The girl snapped at me: 'Is this lug your partner?'

I didn't answer. Her face flushed slowly and her eyes burned. Madder put a hand out and fussed:

'Now listen, Carol, now listen here. This sort of act ain't
32 the way –'

'Shut up!'

'Yeah,' Madder said in a clogged voice. 'Sure.'

Sunset looked the girl over lazily for the third or fourth time. His gunhand rested easily against his hip bone and his whole attitude was of complete relaxation. Having seen him pull his gun once I hoped the girl wasn't fooled.

He said slowly: 'We've heard about you two. What's your offer? I wouldn't listen even, only I can't stand a shooting rap.'

The girl said: 'There's enough in it for four.' Madder nodded his big head vigorously, almost managed a smile.

Sunset glanced at me. I nodded. 'Four it is,' he sighed. 'But that's the top. We'll go to my place and gargle. I don't like it here.'

'We must look simple,' the girl said nastily.

'Kill-simple,' Sunset drawled. 'I've met lots of them. That's why we're going to talk it over. It's not a shooting play.'

Carol Donovan slipped a suede bag from under her left arm and tucked her .32 into it. She smiled. She was pretty when she smiled.

'My ante is in,' she said quietly. 'I'll play. Where is the place?'

'Out Water Street. We'll go in a hack.'

'Lead on, sport.'

We went out of the room and down in the elevator, four friendly people walking out through a lobby full of antlers and stuffed birds and pressed wildflowers in glass frames. The taxi went out Capitol Way, past the square, past a big red apartment house that was too big for the town except when the Legislature was sitting. Along car tracks past the distant capitol buildings and the high closed gates of the governor's mansion.

Oak trees bordered the sidewalks. A few largish residences showed behind garden walls. The taxi shot past them and veered on to a road that led towards the tip of the Sound. In a short while a house showed in a narrow clearing between tall trees. Water glistened far back behind the tree trunks. The house had a roofed porch, a small lawn rotten with weeds and overgrown bushes. There was a shed at the end of a dirt driveway and an antique touring car squatted under the shed.

We got out and I paid the taxi. All four of us carefully watched it out of sight. Then Sunset said:

'My place is upstairs. There's a schoolteacher lives down below. She ain't at home. Let's go up and gargle.'

We crossed the lawn to the porch and Sunset threw a door open, pointed up narrow steps.

'Ladies first. Lead on, beautiful. Nobody locks a door in this town.'

The girl gave him a cool glance and passed him to go up the stairs. I went next, then Madder, Sunset last.

The single room that made up most of the second floor was dark from the trees, had a dormer window, a wide day-bed pushed back under the slope of the roof, a table, some wicker chairs, a small radio, and a round black stove in the middle of
the floor.

Sunset drifted into a kitchenette and came back with a square bottle and some glasses. He poured drinks, lifted one and left the others on the table.

We helped ourselves and sat down.

Sunset put his drink down in a lump, leaned over to put his glass on the floor and came up with his Colt out.

I heard Madder's gulp in the sudden cold silence. The girl's mouth twitched as if she were going to laugh. Then she leaned forward, holding her glass on top of her bag with her left hand.

Sunset slowly drew his lips into a thin straight line. He said slowly and carefully:

'Feet-burners, huh? Burned my pal's feet, huh?'

Madder choked, started to spread his fat hands. The Colt flicked at him. He put his hands on his knees and clutched his kneecaps.

'And suckers at that,' Sunset went on tiredly. 'Burn a guy's feet to make him sing and then walk right into the parlour of one of his pals. You couldn't tie that with Christmas ribbon.'

Madder said jerkily: 'All r-right. W-what's the p-pay-off?' The girl smiled slightly but she didn't say anything.

Sunset grinned. 'Rope,' he said softly. 'A lot of rope tied in hard knots, with water on it. Then me and my pal trundle off to catch fireflies – pearls to you – and when we come back –' he stopped, drew his left hand across the front of his throat. 'Like the idea?' he glanced at me.

'Yeah, but don't make a song about it,' I said. 'Where's the rope?'

'Bureau,' Sunset answered, and pointed with one ear at the corner.

I started in that direction, by way of the walls. Madder made a sudden thin whimpering noise and his eyes turned up in his head and he fell straight forward off the chair on his face, in a dead faint.

That jarred Sunset. He hadn't expected anything so foolish. His right hand jerked around until the Colt was pointing down at Madder's back.

The girl slipped her hand under her bag. The bag lifted an inch. The gun that was caught there in a trick clip – the gun that Sunset thought was inside the bag – spat and flamed briefly.

Sunset coughed. His Colt boomed and a piece of wood detached itself from the back of the chair Madder had been sitting in. Sunset dropped the Colt and put his chin down on his chest and tried to look at the ceiling. His long legs slid out in front of him and his heels made a rasping sound on the floor. He sat like that, limp, his chin on his chest, his eyes looking upward. Dead as a pickled walnut.

I kicked Miss Donovan's chair out from under her and she banged down on her side in a swirl of silken legs. Her hat went crooked on her head. She yelped. I stood on her hand and then shifted suddenly and kicked her gun clear across the attic. I sent her bag after it – with her other gun inside it. She screamed at me.

'Get up,' I snarled.

She got up slowly, backed away from me biting her lip, savage-eyed, suddenly a nasty-faced little brat at bay. She kept on backing until the wall stopped her. Her eyes glittered in a ghastly face.

I glanced down at Madder, went over to a closed door. A bathroom was behind it. I reversed a key and gestured at the girl.

'In.'

She walked stiff-legged across the floor and passed in front of me, almost touching me.

'Listen a minute, shamus —'

I pushed her through the door and slammed it and turned the key. It was all right with me if she wanted to jump out of the window. I had seen the windows from below.

I went across to Sunset, felt him, felt the small hard lump of keys on a ring in his pocket, and got them out without quite knocking him off his chair. I didn't look for anything else.

There were car keys on the ring.

I looked at Madder again, noticed that his fingers were as white as snow. I went down the narrow dark stairs to the porch, around to the side of the house and got into the old touring car under the shed. One of the keys on the ring fitted its ignition lock.

The car took a beating before it started up and let me back it down the dirt driveway to the kerb. Nothing moved in the house that I saw or heard. The tall pines behind and beside the house stirred their upper branches listlessly and a cold heartless sunlight sneaked through them intermittently as they moved.

I drove back to Capitol Way and downtown again as fast

as I dared, past the square and the *Snoqualmie Hotel* and over
the bridge towards the Pacific Ocean and Westport.

9

An hour's fast driving through thinned-out timberland, inter-
rupted by three stops for water and punctuated by the cough
of a head gasket leak, brought me within sound of surf. The
broad white road, striped with yellow down the centre, swept
around the flank of a hill, a distinct cluster of buildings
loomed up in front of the shine of the ocean, and the road
forked. The left fork was sign-posted: 'Westport – 9 Miles',
and didn't go towards the buildings. It crossed a rusty
cantilever bridge and plunged into a region of wind-distorted
apple orchards.

Twenty minutes more and I chugged into Westport, a
sandy spit of land with scattered frame houses dotted over
rising ground behind it. The end of the spit was a long
narrow pier, and the end of the pier a cluster of sailing boats
with half-lowered sails flapping against their single masts.
And beyond them a buoyed channel and a long irregular line
where the water creamed on a hidden sandbar.

Beyond the sandbar the Pacific rolled over to Japan. This
was the last outpost of the coast, the farthest west a man
could go and still be on the mainland of the United States. A
swell place for an ex-convict to hide out with a couple of
somebody else's pearls the size of new potatoes – if he didn't
have any enemies.

I pulled up in front of a cottage that had a sign in the yard: 'Luncheons, Teas, Dinners'. A small rabbit-faced man with freckles was waving a garden rake at two black chickens. The chickens appeared to be sassing him back. He turned when the engine of Sunset's car coughed itself still.

I got out, went through a wicket gate, pointed to the sign. 'Luncheon ready?'

He threw the rake at the chickens, wiped his hands on his trousers and leered. 'The wife put that up,' he confided to me in a thin, impish voice. 'Ham and eggs is what it means.'

'Ham and eggs get along with me,' I said.

We went into the house. There were three tables covered with patterned oilcloth, some chromos on the walls, a full-rigged ship in a bottle on the mantel. I sat down. The host went away through a swing door and somebody yelled at him and a sizzling noise was heard from the kitchen. He came back and leaned over my shoulder, put some cutlery and a paper napkin on the oilcloth.

'Too early for apple brandy, ain't it?' he whispered.

I told him how wrong he was. He went away again and came back with glasses and a quart of clear amber fluid. He sat down with me and poured. A rich baritone voice in the kitchen was singing 'Chloe' over the sizzling.

We clinked glasses and drank and waited for the heat to crawl up our spines.

'Stranger, ain't you?' the little man asked.

I said I was.

'From Seattle maybe? That's a nice piece of goods you got on.'

'Seattle,' I agreed.

'We don't git many strangers,' he said, looking at my left ear. 'Ain't on the way to nowheres. Now before repeal –' he stopped, shifted his sharp, woodpecker gaze to my other ear.

'Ah, before repeal,' I said with a large gesture, and drank knowingly.

He leaned over and breathed on my chin. 'Hell, you could load up in any fish stall on the pier. The stuff come in under catches of crabs and oysters. Hell, Westport was lousy with it. They give the kids cases of Scotch to play with. There wasn't a car in this town that slept in a garage, mister. The garages was all full to the roof of Canadian hooch. Hell, they had a coastguard cutter off the pier watchin' the boats unload one day every week. Friday. Always the same day.' He winked.

I puffed a cigarette and the sizzling noise and the baritone rendering of 'Chloe' went on in the kitchen.

'But hell, you wouldn't be in the liquor business,' he said.

'Hell, no, I'm a goldfish buyer,' I said.

'Okay,' he said sulkily.

I poured us another round of the apple brandy. 'This bottle is on me,' I said. 'And I'm taking a couple more with me.'

He brightened up. 'What did you say the name was?'

'Carmady. You think I'm kidding you about the goldfish. I'm not.'

'Hell, there ain't a livin' in them little fellers, is there?'

I held my sleeve out. 'You said it was a nice piece of

goods. Sure there's a living out of the fancy brands. New brands, new types all the time. My information is there's an old guy down here somewhere that has a real collection. Maybe would sell it. Some he's bred himself.'

I poured us another round of the apple brandy. A large woman with a moustache kicked the swing door open a foot and yelled: 'Pick up the ham and eggs!'

My host scuttled across and came back with my food. I ate. He watched me minutely. After a time he suddenly smacked his skinny leg under the table.

'Old Wallace,' he chuckled. 'Sure, you come to see old Wallace. Hell, we don't know him right well. He don't act neighbourly.'

He turned around in his chair and pointed out through the sleazy curtains at a distant hill. On top of the hill was a yellow and white house that shone in the sun.

'Hell, that's where he lives. He's got a mess of them. Goldfish, huh? Hell, you could bend me with an eye-dropper.'

That ended my interest in the little man. I gobbled my food, paid off for it and for three quarts of apple brandy at a dollar a quart, shook hands and went back out to the touring car.

There didn't seem to be any hurry. Rush Madder would come out of his faint, and he would turn the girl loose. But they didn't know anything about Westport. Sunset hadn't mentioned the name in their presence. They didn't know it when they reached Olympia, or they would have gone there at once. And if they had listened outside my room at the 41 hotel, they would have known I wasn't alone. They hadn't acted as if they knew that when they charged in.

I had lots of time. I drove down to the pier and looked it over. It looked tough. There were fishstalls, drinking dives, a tiny honkytonk for the fishermen, a pool-room, an arcade of slot machines, and smutty peep-shows. Bait fish squirmed and darted in big wooden tanks down in the water along the piles. There were loungers and they looked like trouble for anyone that tried to interfere with them. I didn't see any law enforcement around.

I drove back up the hill to the yellow and white house. It stood very much alone, four blocks from the next nearest dwelling. There were flowers in front, a trimmed green lawn, a rock garden. A woman in a brown and white print dress was popping at aphids with a spray-gun.

I let my heap stall itself, got out and took my hat off.

'Mister Wallace live here?'

She had a handsome face, quiet, firm-looking. She nodded.

'Would you like to see him?' She had a quiet firm voice, a good accent.

It didn't sound like the voice of a train-robber's wife.

I gave her my name, said I'd been hearing about his fish down in the town. I was interested in fancy goldfish.

She put the spray-gun down and went into the house. Bees buzzed around my head, large fuzzy bees that wouldn't mind the cold wind off the sea. Far off like background music the surf pounded on the sandbars. The northern sunshine seemed bleak to me, had no heat in the core of it.

The woman came out of the house and held the door open.

'He's at the top of the stairs,' she said, 'if you'd like to go up.'

I went past a couple of rustic rockers and into the house of the man who had stolen the Leander pearls.

10

Fish tanks were all around the big room, two tiers of them on braced shelves, big oblong tanks with metal frames, some with lights over them and some with lights down in them. Water grasses were festooned in careless patterns behind the algae-coated glass and the water held a ghostly greenish light and through the greenish light moved fish of all the colours of the rainbow.

There were long slim fish like golden darts and Japanese Veiltails with fantastic trailing tails, and X-ray fish as transparent as coloured glass, tiny guppies half an inch long, calico popeyes spotted like a bride's apron, and big lumbering Chinese Moors with telescope eyes, froglike faces and unnecessary fins, waddling through the green water like fat men going to lunch.

Most of the light came from a big sloping skylight. Under the skylight at a bare wooden table a tall gaunt man stood with a squirming red fish in his left hand, and in his right hand a safety razor blade backed with adhesive tape.

He looked at me from under wide grey eyebrows. His eyes were sunken, colourless, opaque. I went over beside him and looked down at the fish he was holding.

43

'Fungus?' I asked.

He nodded slowly. 'White fungus.' He put the fish down on the table and carefully spread its dorsal fin. The fin was ragged and split and the ragged edges had a mossy white colour.

'White fungus,' he said, 'ain't so bad. I'll trim this feller up and he'll be right as rain. What can I do for you, Mister?'

I rolled a cigarette around in my fingers and smiled at him.

'Like people,' I said. 'The fish, I mean. They get things wrong with them.'

He held the fish against the wood and trimmed off the ragged part of the fin. He spread the tail and trimmed that. The fish had stopped squirming.

'Some you can cure,' he said, 'and some you can't. You can't cure swimming-bladder disease, for instance.' He glanced up at me. 'This don't hurt him, case you think it does,' he said. 'You can shock a fish to death but you can't hurt it like a person.'

He put the razor blade down and dipped a cotton swab in some purplish liquid, painted the cut places. Then he dipped a finger in a jar of white vaseline and smeared that over. He dropped the fish in a small tank off to one side of the room. The fish swam around peacefully, quite content.

The gaunt man wiped his hands, sat down at the edge of a bench and stared at me with lifeless eyes. He had been good-looking once, a long time ago.

'You interested in fish?' he asked. His voice had the quiet
careful murmur of the cell block and the exercise yard.

I shook my head. 'Not particularly. That was just an excuse. I came a long way to see you, Mister Sype.'

He moistened his lips and went on staring at me. When his voice came again it was tired and soft.

'Wallace is the name, Mister.'

I puffed a smoke ring and poked my finger through it. 'For my job it's got to be Sype.'

He leaned forward and dropped his hands between his spread bony knees, clasped them together. Big gnarled hands that had done a lot of hard work in their time. His head tipped up at me and his dead eyes were cold under the shaggy brows. But his voice stayed soft.

'Haven't seen a dick in a year. To talk to. What's your lay?'

'Guess,' I said.

His voice got still softer. 'Listen, dick. I've got a nice home here, quiet. Nobody bothers me any more. Nobody's got a right to. I got a pardon straight from the White House. I've got the fish to play with and a man gets fond of anything he takes care of. I don't owe the world a nickel. I paid up. My wife's got enough dough for us to live on. All I want is to be left alone, dick.' He stopped talking, shook his head once. 'You can't burn me up – not any more.'

I didn't say anything. I smiled a little and watched him.

'Nobody can touch me,' he said. 'I got a pardon straight from the President's study. I just want to be let alone.'

I shook my head and kept on smiling at him. 'That's the one thing you can never have – until you give in.'

'Listen,' he said softly. 'You may be new on this case. It's   45 kind of fresh to you. You want to make a rep for yourself. But me, I've had almost twenty years of it, and so have a lot of other people, some of 'em pretty smart people too. *They* know I don't have nothing that don't belong to me. Never did have. Somebody else got it.'

'The mail clerk,' I said. 'Sure.'

'Listen,' he said, still softly. 'I did my time. I know all the angles. I know they ain't going to stop wondering – long as anybody's alive that remembers. I know they're going to send some punk out once in a while to kind of stir it up. That's okay. No hard feelings. Now what do I do to get you to go home again?'

I shook my head and stared past his shoulder at the fish drifting in their big silent tanks. I felt tired. The quiet of the house made ghosts in my brain, ghosts of a lot of years ago. A train pounding through the darkness, a stickup hidden in a mail car, a gun flash, a dead clerk on the floor, a silent drop off at some water tank, a man who had kept a secret for nineteen years – almost kept it.

'You made one mistake,' I said slowly. 'Remember a fellow named Peeler Mardo?'

He lifted his head. I could see him searching in his memory. The name didn't seem to mean anything to him.

'A fellow you knew in Leavenworth,' I said. 'A little runt that was in there for splitting twenty-dollar bills and putting phony backs on them.'

'Yeah,' he said. 'I remember.'

'You told him you had the pearls,' I said.

I could see he didn't believe me. 'I must have been kidding him,' he said slowly, emptily.

'Maybe. But here's the point. He didn't think so. He was up in this country a while ago with a pal, a guy who called himself Sunset. They saw you somewhere and Peeler recognized you. He got to thinking how he could make himself some jack. But he was a coke-hound and he talked in his sleep. A girl got wise and then another girl and a shyster. Peeler got his feet burned and he's dead.'

Sype stared at me unblinkingly. The lines at the corners of his mouth deepened.

I waved my cigarette and went on:

'We don't know how much he told, but the shyster and a girl are in Olympia. Sunset's in Olympia, only he's dead. They killed him. I don't know if they know where you are or not. But they will sometime, or others like them. You can wear the cops down, if they can't find the pearls and you don't try to sell them. You can wear the insurance company down and even the postal men.'

Sype didn't move a muscle. His big knotty hands clenched between his knees didn't move. His dead eyes just stared.

'But you can't wear the chiselers down,' I said. 'They'll never lay off. There'll always be a couple or three with time enough and money enough and meanness enough to bear down. They'll find out what they want to know some way. They'll snatch your wife or take you out in the woods and give you the works. And you'll have to come through . . . Now I've got a decent, square proposition.'

47

'Which bunch are you?' Sype asked suddenly. 'I thought you smelled of dick, but I ain't so sure now.'

'Insurance,' I said. 'Here's the deal. Twenty-five-grand reward in all. Five grand to the girl that passed me the info. She got it on the square and she's entitled to that cut. Ten grand to me. I've done all the work and looked into all the guns. Ten grand to you, through me. You couldn't get a nickel direct. Is there anything in it? How does it look?'

'It looks fine,' he said gently. 'Except for one thing. I don't have no pearls, dick.'

I scowled at him. That was my wad. I didn't have any more. I straightened away from the wall and dropped a cigarette end on the wood floor, crushed it out. I turned to go.

He stood up and put a hand out. 'Wait a minute,' he said gravely, 'and I'll prove it to you.'

He went across the floor in front of me and out of the room. I stared at the fish and chewed my lip. I heard the sound of a car engine somewhere, not very close. I heard a drawer open and shut, apparently in a near-by room.

Sype came back into the fish room. He had a shiny Colt .45 in his gaunt fist. It looked as long as a man's forearm.

He pointed it at me and said: 'I got pearls in this, six of them. Lead pearls. I can comb a fly's whiskers at sixty yards. You ain't no dick. Now get up and blow – and tell your red-hot friends I'm ready to shoot their teeth out any day of the week and twice on Sunday.'

I didn't move. There was a madness in the man's dead eyes. I didn't dare move.

'That's grandstand stuff,' I said slowly. 'I can prove I'm a dick. You're an ex-con and it's felony just having that rod. Put it down and talk sense.'

The car I had heard seemed to be stopping outside the house. Brakes whined on drums. Feet clattered up a walk, up steps. Sudden sharp voices, a caught exclamation.

Sype backed across the room until he was between the table and a big twenty or thirty gallon tank. He grinned at me, the wide clear grin of a fighter at bay.

'I see your friends kind of caught up with you,' he drawled. 'Take your gat out and drop it on the floor while you still got time – and breath.'

I didn't move. I looked at the wiry hair above his eyes. I looked into his eyes. I knew if I moved – even to do what he told me – he would shoot.

Steps came up the stairs. They were clogged, shuffling steps, with a hint of struggle in them.

Three people came into the room.

I I

Mrs Sype came in first, stiff-legged, her eyes glazed, her arms bent rigidly at the elbows and the hands clawing straight forward at nothing, feeling for something that wasn't there. There was a gun in her back, one of Carol Donovan's small .32s, held efficiently in Carol Donovan's small ruthless hand.

Madder came last. He was drunk, brave from the bottle, 49

flushed and savage. He threw the Smith and Wesson down on me and leered.

Carol Donovan pushed Mrs Sype aside. The older woman stumbled over into the corner and sank down on her knees, blank-eyed.

Sype stared at the Donovan girl. He was rattled because she was a girl and young and pretty. He hadn't been used to the type. Seeing her took the fire out of him. If men had come in he would have shot them to pieces.

The small dark white-faced girl faced him coldly, said in her tight chilled voice:

'All right, Dad. Shed the heater. Make it smooth now.'

Sype leaned down slowly, not taking his eyes off her. He put his enormous frontier Colt on the floor.

'Kick it away from you, Dad.'

Sype kicked it. The gun skidded across the bare boards, over towards the centre of the room.

'That's the way, old-timer. You hold on him, Rush, while I unrod the dick.'

The two guns swivelled and the hard grey eyes were looking at me now. Madder went a little way towards Sype and pointed his Smith and Wesson at Sype's chest.

The girl smiled, not a nice smile. 'Bright boy, eh? You sure stick your neck out all the time, don't you? Made a beef, shamus. Didn't frisk your skinny pal. He had a little map in one shoe.'

'I didn't need one,' I said smoothly, and grinned at her.

I tried to make the grin appealing, because Mrs Sype was moving her knees on the floor, and every move took her nearer to Sype's Colt.

'But you're all washed up now, you and your big smile. Hoist the mitts while I get your iron. Up, Mister.'

She was a girl, about five feet two inches tall, and weighed around a hundred and twenty. Just a girl. I was five-eleven and a half, weighed one-ninety-five. I put my hands up and hit her on the jaw.

That was crazy, but I had all I could stand of the Donovan–Madder act, the Donovan–Madder guns, the Donovan–Madder tough talk. I hit her on the jaw.

She went back a yard and her popgun went off. A slug burned my ribs. She started to fall. Slowly, like a slow-motion picture, she fell. There was something silly about it.

Mrs Sype got the Colt and shot her in the back.

Madder whirled and the instant he turned Sype rushed him. Madder jumped back and yelled and covered Sype again. Sype stopped cold and the wide crazy grin came back on his gaunt face.

The slug from the Colt knocked the girl forward as though a door had whipped in a high wind. A flurry of blue cloth, something thumped my chest – her head. I saw her face for a moment as she bounced back, a strange face that I had never seen before.

Then she was a huddled thing on the floor at my feet, small, deadly, extinct, with redness coming out from under her, and the tall quiet woman behind her with the smoking Colt held in both hands.

Madder shot Sype twice. Sype plunged forward still grinning and hit the end of the table. The purplish liquid he had used on the sick fish sprayed up over him. Madder shot him again as he was falling.

I jerked my Lüger out and shot Madder in the most painful place I could think of that wasn't likely to be fatal – the back of the knee. He went down exactly as if he had tripped over a hidden wire. I had cuffs on him before he even started to groan.

I kicked guns here and there and went over to Mrs Sype and took the big Colt out of her hands.

It was very still in the room for a little while. Eddies of smoke drifted towards the skylight, filmy grey, pale in the afternoon sun. I heard the surf booming in the distance. Then I heard a whistling sound close at hand.

It was Sype trying to say something. His wife crawled across to him, still on her knees, huddled beside him. There was blood on his lips and bubbles. He blinked hard, trying to clear his head. He smiled up at her. His whistling voice said very faintly:

'The Moors, Hattie – the Moors.'

Then his neck went loose and the smile melted off his face. His head rolled to one side on the bare floor.

Mrs Sype touched him, then got very slowly to her feet and looked at me, calm, dry-eyed.

She said in a low clear voice: 'Will you help me carry him to the bed? I don't like him here with these people.'

I said: 'Sure. What was that he said?'

'I don't know. Some nonsense about his fish, I think.'

I lifted Sype's shoulders and she took his feet and we
carried him into the bedroom and put him on the bed. She

folded his hands on his chest and shut his eyes. She went over and pulled the blinds down.

'That's all, thank you,' she said, not looking at me. 'The telephone is downstairs.'

She sat down in a chair beside the bed and put her head down on the coverlet near Sype's arm.

I went out of the room and shut the door.

12

Madder's leg was bleeding slowly, not dangerously. He stared at me with fear-crazed eyes while I tied a tight handkerchief above his knee. I figured he had a cut tendon and maybe a chipped kneecap. He might walk a little lame when they came to hang him.

I went downstairs and stood on the porch looking at the two cars in front, then down the hill towards the pier. Nobody could have told where the shots came from, unless he happened to be passing. Quite likely nobody had even noticed them. There was probably shooting in the woods around there a good deal.

I went back into the house and looked at the crank telephone on the living-room wall, but didn't touch it yet. Something was bothering me. I lit a cigarette and stared out of the window and a ghost voice said in my ears: 'The Moors, Hattie. The Moors.'

I went back upstairs into the fish room. Madder was groaning now, thick panting groans. What did I care about a torturer like Madder?

The girl was quite dead. None of the tanks was hit. The fish swam peacefully in their green water, slow and peaceful and easy. They didn't care about Madder either.

The tank with the black Chinese Moors in it was over in the corner, about ten gallon size. There were just four of them, big fellows, about four inches body length, coal black all over. Two of them were sucking oxygen on top of the water and two were waddling sluggishly on the bottom. They had thick deep bodies with a lot of spreading tail and high dorsal fins and their bulging telescope eyes that made them look like frogs when they were head towards you.

I watched them fumbling around in the green stuff that was growing in the tank. A couple of red pond snails were window-cleaning. The two on the bottom looked thicker and more sluggish than the two on the top. I wondered why.

There was a long-handled strainer made of woven string lying between two of the tanks. I got it and fished down in the tank, trapped one of the big Moors and lifted it out. I turned it over in the net, looked at its faintly silver belly. I saw something that looked like a suture. I felt the place. There was a hard lump under it.

I pulled the other one off the bottom. Same suture, same hard round lump. I got one of the two that had been sucking air on top. No suture, no hard round lump. It was harder to catch too.

I put it back in the tank. My business was with the other two. I like goldfish as well as the next man, but business is business and crime is crime. I took my coat off and rolled my sleeves up and picked the razor blade backed with adhesive off the table.

It was a very messy job. It took about five minutes. Then they lay in the palm of my hand, three-quarters of an inch in diameter, heavy, perfectly round, milky white and shimmering with that inner light no other jewel had. The Leander pearls.

I washed them off, wrapped them in my handkerchief, rolled down my sleeves and put my coat back on. I looked at Madder, at his little pain- and fear-tortured eyes, the sweat on his face. I didn't care anything about Madder. He was a killer, a torturer.

I went out of the fish room. The bedroom door was still shut. I went down below and cranked the wall telephone.

'This is the Wallace place at Westport,' I said. 'There's been an accident. We need a doctor and we'll have to have the police. What can you do?'

The girl said: 'I'll try and get you a doctor, Mr Wallace. It may take a little time though. There's a town marshal at Westport. Will he do?'

'I suppose so,' I said and thanked her and hung up. There were points about a country telephone after all.

I lit another cigarette and sat down in one of the rustic rockers on the porch. In a little while there were steps and Mrs Sype came out of the house. She stood a moment looking off down the hills, then she sat down in the other rocker beside her. Her dry eyes looked at me steadily.

'You're a detective, I suppose,' she said slowly, diffidently.   55

'Yes, I represent the company that insured the Leander pearls.'

She looked off into the distance. 'I thought he would have peace here,' she said. 'That nobody would bother him any more. That this place would be a sort of sanctuary.'

'He ought not to have tried to keep the pearls.'

She turned her head, quickly this time. She looked blank now, then she looked scared.

I reached down in my pocket and got out the wadded handkerchief, opened it up on the palm of my hand. They lay there together on the white linen, two hundred grand worth of murder.

'He could have had his sanctuary,' I said. 'Nobody wanted to take it away from him. But he wasn't satisfied with that.'

She looked slowly, lingeringly at the pearls. Then her lips twitched. Her voice got hoarse.

'Poor Wally,' she said. 'So you did find them. You're pretty clever, you know. He killed dozens of fish before he learned how to do that trick.' She looked up into my face. A little wonder showed at the back of her eyes.

She said: 'I always hated the idea. Do you remember the old Bible theory of the scapegoat?'

I shook my head, no.

'The animal on which the sins of a man were laid and then it was driven off into the wilderness. The fish were his scapegoat.'

She smiled at me. I didn't smile back.

She said, still smiling faintly: 'You see, he once had the

pearls, the real ones, and suffering seemed to him to make them his. But he couldn't have had any profit from them, even if he had found them again. It seems some landmark changed, while he was in prison, and he never could find the spot in Idaho where they were buried.'

An icy finger was moving slowly up and down my spine. I opened my mouth and something I supposed might be my voice said:

'Huh?'

She reached a finger out and touched one of the pearls. I was still holding them out, as if my hand was a shelf nailed to the wall.

'So he got these,' she said. 'In Seattle. They're hollow, filled with white wax. I forget what they call the process. They look very fine. Of course I never saw any really valuable pearls.'

'What did he get them for?' I croaked.

'Don't you see? They were his sin. He had to hide them in the wilderness, this wilderness. He hid them in the fish. And do you know –' she leaned towards me again and her eyes shone. She said very slowly, very earnestly:

'Sometimes I think that in the very end, just the last year or so, he actually believed they were the real pearls he was hiding. Does all this mean anything to you?'

I looked down at my pearls. My hand and the handkerchief closed over them slowly.

I said: 'I'm a plain man, Mrs Sype. I guess the scapegoat idea is a bit over my head. I'd say he was just trying to kid himself a bit – like any heavy loser.'

57

She smiled again. She was handsome when she smiled. Then she shrugged, quite lightly.

'Of course, you would see it that way. But me –' she spread her hands. 'Oh, well, it doesn't matter much now. May I have them for a keepsake?'

'Have them?'

'The – the phony pearls. Surely you don't –'

I stood up. An old Ford roadster without a top was chugging up the hill. A man in it had a big star on his vest. The chatter of the motor was like the chatter of some old angry bald-headed ape in the zoo.

Mrs Sype was standing beside me, with her hand half out, a thin, beseeching look on her face.

I grinned at her with sudden ferocity.

'Yeah, you were pretty good in there for a while,' I said. 'I damn near fell for it. And was I cold down the back lady! But you helped. "Phony" was a shade out of character for you. Your work with the Colt was fast and kind of ruthless. Most of all Sype's last words queered it. "The Moors, Hattie – the Moors." He wouldn't have bothered with that if the stones had been ringers. And he wasn't sappy enough to kid himself all the way.'

For a moment her face didn't change at all. Then it did. Something horrible showed in her eyes. She put her lips out and spat at me. Then she slammed into the house.

I tucked twenty-five thousand dollars into my vest pocket. Twelve thousand five hundred for me and twelve thousand five hundred for Kathy Horne. I could see her eyes when I brought her the cheque, and when she put it in the bank, to wait for Johnny to get paroled from Quentin.

The Ford had pulled up behind the other cars. The man driving spat over the side, yanked his emergency brake on, got out without using the door. He was a big fellow in shirt sleeves.

I went down the steps to meet him.

GABRIEL GARCÍA MÁRQUEZ · *Bon Voyage, Mr President*
PATRICK MCGRATH · *The Angel*
HERMAN MELVILLE · *Bartleby*
SPIKE MILLIGAN · *Gunner Milligan, 954024*
MICHEL DE MONTAIGNE · *Four Essays*
JAN MORRIS · *From the Four Corners*
JOHN MORTIMER · *Rumpole and the Younger Generation*
R. K. NARAYAN · *Tales from Malgudi*
ANAÏS NIN · *A Model*
FRANK O'CONNOR · *The Genius*
GEORGE ORWELL · *Pages from a Scullion's Diary*
CAMILLE PAGLIA · *Sex and Violence, or Nature and Art*
SARA PARETSKY · *A Taste of Life*
EDGAR ALLAN POE · *The Pit and the Pendulum*
MISS READ · *Village Christmas*
JEAN RHYS · *Let Them Call It Jazz*
DAMON RUNYON · *The Snatching of Bookie Bob*
SAKI · *The Secret Sin of Septimus Brope*
WILL SELF · *Scale*
GEORGES SIMENON · *Death of a Nobody*
MURIEL SPARK · *The Portobello Road*
ROBERT LOUIS STEVENSON · *The Pavilion on the Links*
PAUL THEROUX · *Down the Yangtze*
WILLIAM TREVOR · *Matilda's England*
MARK TULLY · *Ram Chander's Story*
JOHN UPDIKE · *Friends from Philadelphia*
EUDORA WELTY · *Why I Live at the P. O.*
EDITH WHARTON · *Madame de Treymes*
OSCAR WILDE · *The Happy Prince*
VIRGINIA WOOLF · *Killing the Angel in the House*

READ MORE IN PENGUIN

For complete information about books available from Penguin and how to order them, please write to us at the appropriate address below. Please note that for copyright reasons the selection of books varies from country to country.

IN THE UNITED KINGDOM: Please write to *Dept. JC, Penguin Books Ltd, FREEPOST, West Drayton, Middlesex UB7 0BR.*

If you have any difficulty in obtaining a title, please send your order with the correct money, plus ten per cent for postage and packaging, to *PO Box No. 11, West Drayton, Middlesex UB7 0BR.*

IN THE UNITED STATES: Please write to *Consumer Sales, Penguin USA, P.O. Box 999, Dept. 17109, Bergenfield, New Jersey 07621-0120.* VISA and MasterCard holders call 1-800-253-6476 to order all Penguin titles.

IN CANADA: Please write to *Penguin Books Canada Ltd, 10 Alcorn Avenue, Suite 300, Toronto, Ontario M4V 3B2.*

IN AUSTRALIA: Please write to *Penguin Books Australia Ltd, P.O. Box 257, Ringwood, Victoria 3134.*

IN NEW ZEALAND: Please write to *Penguin Books (NZ) Ltd, Private Bag 102902, North Shore Mail Centre, Auckland 10.*

IN INDIA: Please write to *Penguin Books India Pvt Ltd, 706 Eros Apartments, 56 Nehru Place, New Delhi 110 019.*

IN THE NETHERLANDS: Please write to *Penguin Books Netherlands bv, Postbus 3507, NL-1001 AH Amsterdam.*

IN GERMANY: Please write to *Penguin Books Deutschland GmbH, Metzlerstrasse 26, 60594 Frankfurt am Main.*

IN SPAIN: Please write to *Penguin Books S. A., Bravo Murillo 19, 1o B, 28015 Madrid.*

IN ITALY: Please write to *Penguin Italia s.r.l., Via Felice Casati 20, I–20124 Milano.*

IN FRANCE: Please write to *Penguin France S. A., 17 rue Lejeune, F–31000 Toulouse.*

IN JAPAN: Please write to *Penguin Books Japan, Ishikiribashi Building, 2–5–4, Suido, Bunkyo-ku, Tokyo 112.*

IN GREECE: Please write to *Penguin Hellas Ltd, Dimocritou 3, GR–106 71 Athens.*

IN SOUTH AFRICA: Please write to *Longman Penguin Southern Africa (Pty) Ltd, Private Bag X08, Bertsham 2013.*